An IFWG Publishing

Tool Tales

Microfiction inspired by antique tools

Photographs by Ellen Datlow

Stories by Kaaron Warren

Tool Tales

All Rights Reserved

ISBN-13: 978-1-922556-01-1

Text Copyright ©2021 Kaaron Warren

Photographs Copyright ©2021 by Ellen Datlow

V1.0

Printed in Palatino Linotype and FreightNeo Pro.

IFWG Publishing International

www.ifwgpublishing.com

*We become what we behold. We shape our tools,
and thereafter our tools shape us.*

–Marshall McLuhan

Tool 1

She found it under her grandfather's bed, hidden beneath a pair of pyjama pants that were stiff with dust. As she held it, the dial quivered and she wondered what it measured.

Her grandfather rattled, breath tearing his throat, and the dial lifted. She felt the tool warm in her palm.

One last breath and he was done.

Her grandfather had DNR tattooed on his chest, but she did resuscitate him momentarily over and over again, because watching the dial rise and fall made her feel a power she had not felt before.

At first he said, "No," and "Please," and "Don't," but then he said, "It's only right," and "This is just," and "True judgement" and she wondered what he'd used this tool for, that he thought he deserved to die and die and die again.

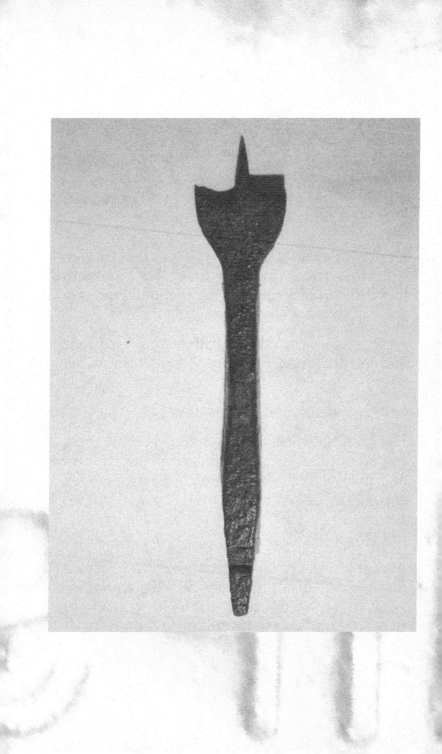

Tool 2

Some are born with a silver spoon; I was born with an iron tool. Half as long as me newborn, there are photos of me with my tiny hand resting on its length. Rust or something similar stains the sheet. Sharp at one end, sharper at the other, my father wrapped the tool in a bunny rug until I was old enough to be careful, or he tucked it under my mattress. That made him nervous, though. Really, he liked me to be in physical contact with the tool at all times.

He told me today the tool had killed a dozen witches. "Mothers, some call them," he said, and he began to train me for the day I might have to kill a witch myself.

Tool 3

I have a collection of beautiful teeth. They aren't my own; I still have my baby teeth, set deep in my gums, unwilling to fall. Xrays show no adult ones waiting, none formed, and no one knows why.

So I take these teeth and I set them all in silver, because they are beautiful but imperfect. They show some decay, some decline like, perhaps, the people they came from. So I set them in silver and when I find the right dentist, he'll pull my baby teeth and settle these beautiful silver teeth in place.

In the meantime I'll practise my smile.

Because first impressions matter.

Tool 4

He was a handsome man. When he danced (traditional, wild, subtle or worshipful, there was nothing he couldn't do) you'd think he was a god. But you don't know what's in a person until you bury them. Leave them ten years. Then dig them up and see what they've become.

A good man is rot and bone.

A bad man stays solid, hoping for a second chance.

The god of dance was turned to iron, frozen in a dance move that used to work for him.

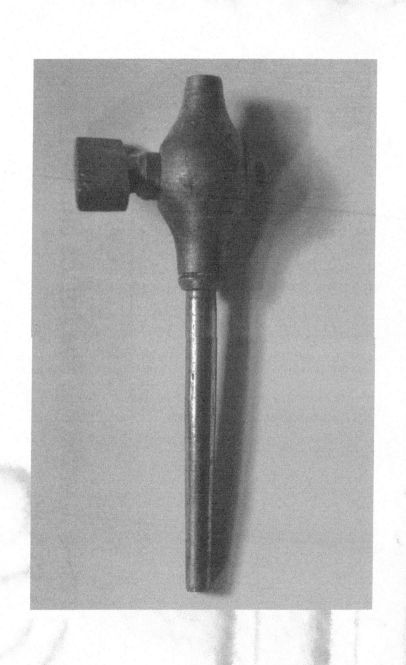

Tool 5

Once, when I was a kid, I turned on all the garden taps in my street. This was a long time ago, when Australia still had running water easy as that.

When we still had water.

I turned each one on only a trickle, so no one noticed until they stepped ankle-deep in the mud that water made.

Not the fastest practical joke, but a good one.

I wish I could laugh now, but my throat is so very dry. And all I can think about are those dripping taps, wasting water, decades ago. And in mind's eye I can see myself, lying in the mud, mouth open.

Drinking.

Tool 6

Edgar found the tool buried in his backyard. An unusually heavy rain storm washed layers of dirt away, revealing many things: Bones buried by a long-ago dog, a child's forgotten toy, and this tool.

Edgar found it handle up and thought it was a small garden fork. The wood was notched and dented in parts, but still he dug around it, because most things are useful in one way or another.

He reached metal. A thick loop sat embedded in the handle, so not a fork. He tugged but it needed more digging out.

Even then, though.

Even when most of the loop was revealed it wouldn't tug loose and he didn't know why until, using all his strength (he was once a much stronger man. That, of all things, was still clear in his mind) he managed to pull it out of the ground.

Tangled around the curve of the loop was a thick, long lock of hair, with roots still attached.

He stared at the hole the tool left behind, knowing he would have to dig, but not wanting to remember whose head this hair once covered.

Tool 7

"Shake the egg," April would call out, curled up in her bed at night, and her mother would shake the perfect wooden egg. The two halves fitted together snug and neat and inside sat a silver thimble that had belonged to April's grandmother. April's mother shook the egg and the gentle rattle of the thimble on wood was a comfort. It meant her mother was close by. Within hearing distance.

They buried April's mother with that egg when she was killed by a sober driver, April's mother not sober, out looking for something she couldn't find at home. April herself closed her mother's fingers over that perfect wooden egg.

She thought she heard the rattle again, lying in a hospital bed with pneumonia.

And again, when a fire started from a faulty heater.

And then, finally, lying on the bathroom floor after a fall (old bones, poor reflexes) she said, "Shake the egg" and she heard the rattle of her mother calling her to comfort.

Tool 8

In this house we all pull our weight. We know what our parents (grandparents, great-grandparents) gave up for us, paying week after week, year after year, sacrificing fancy dinners, second cars, holidays, so we could live in this house. The data tube that passed from generation to generation, kept track of the numbers, sits now in a glass box in the front hall, to remind us of what they did.

We are happy most days, with the cheer of our own children, the many rooms to explore, the beauty of the walls, the thickness of the carpet.

But other days, when in the distance we can hear the noise of strangers, the call of adventure, we wish, with all our hearts, that we could step outside just once.

Tool 9

Big mouth, loud mouth, say a word out of place and in it goes. I've never been able to hold my tongue so I know the feel of wood in my cheeks. My tongue works at the groove, at the hole, until I can taste blood.

Worst is when they screw the thing too high on the wall and I have to stand on my toes, neck stretched.

All the words are in my head, now. But one day, when they aren't listening, I'll get the chance to speak.

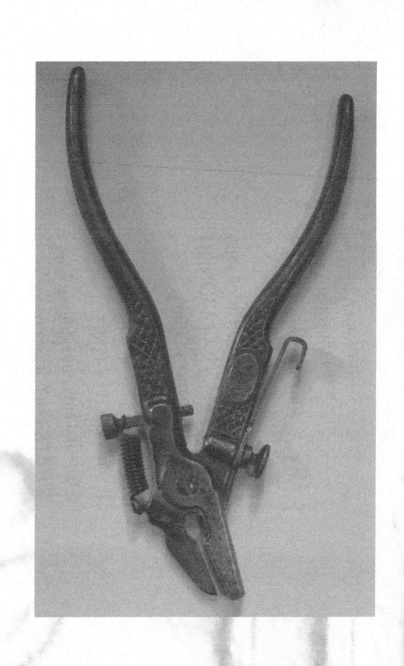

Tool 10

It was dark in his workroom but Ruedigen didn't notice. His eyes were used to the dark by now and if he worked in the shadows, perhaps they would forget he was there? Leave him be another year, or ten? Better to die here, at his bench, than where they wanted to send him.

He knew this was his last tool. "Are you finished?" they asked, and he said, "One more detail." He added a spring, a lever, a hook, another screw, feeling a familiar sense of excitement as he imagined it at work, pinching nostrils closed, pressing fingers flat.

"One more detail," he said, etching fine work into the handles. He tested them. They opened smoothly, closed with a satisfying snick.

"You can bring the tool," they said, surprisingly gently. "No reason why not."

So they walked out, Ruedigen blinking in the sunlight, and he saw that he had not been forgotten at all. The crowd brandished his beautiful tools (the self-timer, the auger bit, the iron pliers, the gas valve, the button hook, so many more), some smiling, many angry at what he had wrought.

Those many cheered as they used his tools against him in a very public execution.

About Tool Tales

Tool Tales came out of a Twitter conversation between us a few years ago, about the collecting of objects and why we loved not only the process, but the stories these objects told. Ellen talked about some of the strange tools she had lying around her apartment and wondered if anyone on Facebook would like to see them. I volunteered to write a microstory for each one! Ellen told me nothing about the object, and I wasn't allowed to look it up.

As Ellen said at the time, "We'll continue until one or both of us get sick of it or have no time. One thing that won't happen-is us having objects/tools around to post." We stopped at ten; it seemed the right number.

The Tools

Tool 1.

I discovered that this is a "Vintage Self Timer for cameras made by Haka in Germany c.1930s. The typeface on the top of the object reads "Autoknips II-made in Germany.

Tool 2.

A six inch long very old Auger bit (drill) for a bit brace (thanks to Bruce Bouldry for the ID).

Tool 3.

Four metal teeth. These four teeth were found by me in a local thrift shop that had a bowlful of them—all different shapes. I was told they're lead but I doubt that because I see nothing on google about anyone ever making lead teeth. In fact, I find nothing on google resembling them. More information would be lovely.

Tool 4.

A rusted iron plier, about six inches long. No idea what it's specifically for.

Whit Pond says: Found another one even closer in design, though this one actually has a screwdriver added as well. Generally described as "vintage multi-tool". Also, I'd say the one in your picture may have been a custom forged job rather than a manufactured one.

Tool 5.

Stu Segal says: This looks like the valve from an old-fashioned natural gas line in a home. You know, early 20th century pre-electric lights, when gas lines ran through houses and were used for lighting. (We lived in a house that was built in 1901, and there were gas lines in the walls and valves everywhere.)

With a hallmark that looks like H star R or E

Tool 6.

Antique button hook for shoes identified by Gwyndyn Alexander.

Tool 7.

The egg—I assume a darning egg with thimble inside.

Tool 8.

Metal cylinder. Whitt Pond says: Well, it's got an old computer punch card wrapped around it, and the fastenings seem to indicate that it was made to hold such a card. Might have been part of a very old card reader apparatus, but I'm guessing.

Tool 9.

Multi tool with no bits.

Tool 10.

This was in fact the very first tool that got me started collecting them. I bought it at Convent Garden's Monday antique market. The seller didn't know what it was for and I never knew until reader Zane Melder found one like it on ebay: Antique Nipper-Tool-Pliers-Adjust-Teeth-Saw-Hacksaw